Going to a
HORSE FARM

by Shirley Kerby James

illustrated by Laura Jacques

 Charlesbridge

Published by
Charlesbridge Publishing
85 Main Street
Watertown, MA 02172-4411
(617) 926-0329

Library of Congress
Catalog Card Number 91-77782
ISBN 0-88106-476-9 (softcover)
ISBN 0-88106-477-7 (trade hardcover)

Printed in the United States of America
(sc) 10 9 8 7 6 5 4 3 2
(hc) 10 9 8 7 6 5 4 3 2 1

Printed on Recycled Paper.

There is a great excitement at Mr. Roy's horse farm. In the barn, a new baby foal has just been born. Mr. Roy's daughter Sally says, "Hooray! A new foal! May I invite Paula and her brother Tony to come see it?"

"Yes," says Mr. Roy.

Paula and Tony are thrilled. On the way up to the stables they see three horses eating grass in a field.

"They must eat a lot of grass," says Paula, "because they are all very fat."

"These horses look fat because they are about to have babies," Mr. Roy explains. "Their babies will be born in a few weeks' time. These mares eat special food and vitamins as well as grass."

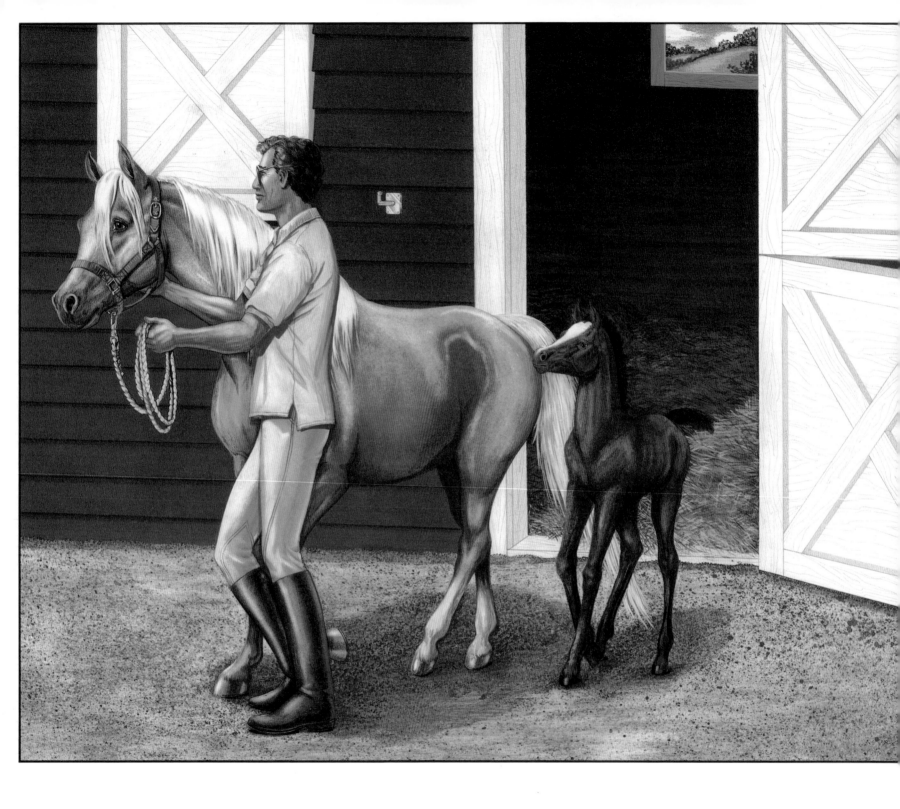

Then Paula and Tony see the tiny foal. She is only five days old, but her thin legs are as long as her mother's. She could stand up and walk one hour after she was born.

The foal is wearing her own tiny head collar. When Mr. Roy leads her with one hand, he puts his other arm round her back to steady her. She must learn to be led quietly before she gets too big and strong.

The foal can move really fast! She stays close to her mother's side all the time. Her long legs help her keep up with her mother when she runs.

The foal has a drink of milk whenever she likes. Her mother needs to produce a lot of milk.

When a mother doesn't have enough milk, the foal has to be fed from a baby bottle! That's a lot of work because she is thirsty every 20 minutes.

The foal needs to rest a lot, too. She lies down in the grass to nap. Paula and Tony laugh as the foal tries to control her long legs.

The children watch a young horse who is only two years old. He is being schooled on a long line called a lunge. He is learning to obey the trainer's voice.

Then it is time for a three year old stallion to be trained.

"We don't ride the horses until they are three and have most of their growth.
Then they're strong enough to carry our weight," Mr. Roy explains.

The stallion knows how to move quietly on the lunge and obey the trainer's commands. As soon as he gets used to a saddle, he will learn to accept the weight of a rider on his back. A rider uses the reins and the pressure of his or her legs to tell the horse what to do.

"We always praise our horses when they do well," says Mr. Roy. He strokes the stallion's neck and feeds him an apple, which is the stallion's favorite treat.

Sally leads an old mare called Smokey from the paddock. Smokey is twenty-five years old and is very quiet and gentle. Sally is allowed to ride Smokey whenever she likes.

Sally shows Paula and Tony how to brush Smokey. The old mare likes to be brushed, and she doesn't move.

"You can tell she's old because she's all white," says Paula.

"Smokey was white when she was young," says Sally. "You can tell her age by her teeth! As horses get older, their teeth get longer and longer."

Mr. Roy is very careful when he puts the bit into Smokey's mouth. He doesn't want to hurt her. Tony wants to see Smokey's long teeth!

The saddle fits comfortably on Smokey's back.

The red saddle blanket underneath is thick and soft, and it stops the saddle from slipping. The girth strap holds the saddle firmly in place.

Sally asks Paula if she wants to ride. Does she!

Mr. Roy lifts Paula onto Smokey's back.

Then he makes the stirrups the right length for Paula's legs
and shows her how to hold the reins.

Paula feels high above the ground.

She takes a deep breath as Smokey begins to walk.

Smokey's body moves up and down, and Paula is rocked about in the saddle.

"Me too! Me too!" shouts Tony. "Can I have a ride, too?"

"Sure you can," says Mr. Roy, "but please talk quietly around Smokey. Horses get nervous when they hear loud noises."

Tony sits on Smokey's back. He feels a little scared when he looks down.

Mr. Roy asks, "Did you know horses wear different size shoes just like people?"

"No," says Tony, "I didn't. What size does Smokey wear?"

"Size one," says Mr. Roy.

"So do I!" laughs Tony, and he pats Smokey's neck.

Sally rides Smokey next. She has been riding for a long time, and she knows how to sit quietly when Smokey gallops. She moves only from the waist up, without bouncing out of the saddle.

Sally has been learning to jump on Smokey. She leans forward so that she doesn't lose her balance when Smokey lands.

Smokey has behaved well with the children. She deserves a special treat.
"Let's give her a carrot," says Sally. "That's her favorite food."

It is time to prepare the stable for the night. The stalls are cleaned, and soft beds of woodshavings or straw are put down for the horses.

The horses need fresh water to drink all the time. Sally likes to help in the
stables at feeding time.

Mr. Roy measures out oats and wheat bran and corn for the horses. This food gives them the vitamins and minerals they need.

Horses are grazing animals so they like to eat most of the time. That's why Mr. Roy also gives them large amounts of hay to eat. Sally, Paula, and Tony help carry hay to the stalls.

The new foal shares the large loose box stall with her mother. The bedding is piled high around the walls so that she won't get hurt. She will live with her mother until she is six months old. Then she will share a field with the older foals.

The older foals like to run and play. While they're having fun, running helps them grow strong and healthy. Sally points to the foals and says, "There's Blaze, and Shadow, and Ranger, and Star."

"You must come back next week and help us name the new foal," says Sally.

Paula says, "That would be great!" On the way home, she thinks 'Wobbly' would be a good name because the foal is so wobbly when it stands up.

Maybe you can think of a good name, too.